MARY-KATE A... IN ACTION!

Fast Food Fight

A novelization by Alexa Rose
based on the teleplay
by Robin Riordan

HarperEntertainment
An Imprint of HarperCollins*Publishers*

A PARACHUTE PRESS BOOK

A PARACHUTE PRESS BOOK

Parachute Publishing, L.L.C.
156 Fifth Avenue, Suite 302
New York, NY 10010

Published by
⚑HarperEntertainment
An Imprint of HarperCollins*Publishers*
10 East 53rd Street, New York, NY 10022-5299

ISBN 0-06-009309-9

HarperCollins®, ⚑®, and HarperEntertainment™ are trademarks of HarperCollins Publishers Inc.

First printing: October 2003

Printed in China

Visit the on-line book boutique on the World Wide Web at
www.mary-kateandashley.com.

Visit HarperEntertainment on the World Wide Web at
www.harpercollins.com

10 9 8 7 6 5 4 3 2 1

CHAPTER ONE

Really Fast Food

"Thanks for bringing us to your aunt and uncle's restaurant, Rod," Ashley said.

"We love this place," Mary-Kate said. "It has the best Chinese food in town!"

"Plus they don't make me pay full price!" Rod added.

Mary-Kate and Ashley were sisters and

special agents. Rod was a special agent, too. They all worked for a top-secret group called Headquarters.

Mary-Kate and Ashley's job was to protect the world from villains. Rod's job was to drive the girls wherever they needed to go. But today the teenagers weren't planning on saving the world. Their only mission was to eat lunch!

"All this talk is making me extra hungry," Quincy said. He was Mary-Kate and Ashley's beige Scottish terrier.

To everyone else Quincy looked like an ordinary dog. But he was really a robot with a computer inside him! He helped Mary-Kate and Ashley on their missions.

"Shhh! Quincy, be quiet!" Ashley said. "No one is supposed to know that you can talk, remember?"

Quincy put one paw over his mouth. "Sorry," he whispered.

The four friends strolled up to the Chow Family Restaurant. A large crowd stood outside.

"Wow, look at all these people!" Mary-Kate said. "We're going to have to wait a long time for a table."

Ashley glanced up the street. "Uh, Mary-Kate, I think the line is for that

restaurant over there." She pointed toward the restaurant next door.

"Whoa!" Mary-Kate said. "That restaurant wasn't there last week. Where did it come from?"

"I don't know, but it sure is ugly." Ashley giggled. The restaurant was made of shiny steel. Bright lights in the shapes of tacos and Chinese food boxes hung from the windows. A giant plastic hamburger stood next to the door.

"I don't get it," Mary-Kate said. "Do they serve Mexican food, American food, *and* Chinese food? I've never been to a restaurant that serves so many different kinds of food."

Ashley shrugged. "Beats me." She stepped inside the Chow Family Restaurant. It was completely empty. There wasn't a customer in sight!

"What's going on here?" Mary-Kate

asked as they all sat down. "This place is usually packed!"

"Does this mean more food for us?" Quincy asked. "I hope so! Bring on the lunch—and hold the sesame seeds!" He grabbed a fortune cookie out of a big bowl in the middle of the table. Quincy hated sesame seeds. They were the only food he wouldn't eat.

Whoosh! The kitchen door swung open. A woman with dark curly hair

rushed out. It was Jane Chow, Rod's aunt.
Behind her was Frank Chow, Rod's uncle.

"Rodney! Girls!" Aunt Jane said.
"Thank goodness you're here!"

"Where is everyone?" Rod asked.

"They're all eating at Quick Food, the
new restaurant next door," Uncle Frank
said.

Aunt Jane waved a hand at a TV sitting
on a nearby counter. "There are reports

about Quick Food all over the news," she said. "Look! There's one now."

Ashley stared at the television. On the screen a reporter stood next to two boys. They didn't look much older than Mary-Kate and Ashley. One boy was tall with dark brown hair and green eyes. The other was short with light brown hair and brown eyes.

"I'm here with Donnie and Danny Richards, owners of the new Quick Food restaurant," the reporter said into the camera. She turned to the boys. "You two sure are busy!"

"That's right," Danny said. "Our mom and dad bought us this restaurant. Donnie and I have been working together to make it super-popular."

"You can say that again," the reporter said. "This restaurant is *so* popular, it has been taking business away from everyone else."

"That's right. Danny and I want to make our parents proud," Donnie said. "We're going to make sure Quick Food is the only restaurant that anyone *ever* goes to. First we're going to take over all the other restaurants on this block."

"Then we're going to take over all the restaurants in the state," Danny added. "Pretty soon, Quick Food will be the only place to eat in the entire country!"

"And how do you plan to do that?" the reporter asked.

"We can't tell you," Donnie said.

"But once people eat our food," Danny said, "they can't help coming back for more!" He smiled an evil smile.

Uh-oh, Ashley thought. *I've seen that look before . . . on some of the worst villains Mary-Kate and I have ever faced!*

She turned to her sister. "I don't like the sound of this."

"Me, neither," Mary-Kate agreed. "Danny and Donnie are definitely trouble!"

"Looks like we have a new mission," Ashley said.

Mary-Kate nodded. "To save the restaurant world from Danny and Donnie Richards!"

CHAPTER TWO
A Taste of Trouble

"So, what's our first step?" Ashley asked.

Mary-Kate shrugged. "I'm not sure," she said. "Quincy, what do you think we should do?"

"Maybe my fortune cookie will give us a clue," Quincy said. He smashed his

cookie with one paw and pulled out a tiny slip of paper. "'Knowledge is power,'" he read.

Ashley nodded. "Good thinking. Let's find out everything we can about Quick Food."

"All right!" Mary-Kate slapped Ashley a high five. "Special Agents Misty and Amber are on the case!"

Ashley smiled. Mary-Kate loved using their special-agent names—almost as much as she loved using their high-tech gadgets!

"Hey," Rod said. "I know who can get us the information we need—IQ!"

Fifteen-year-old Ivan Quintero also worked at Headquarters. His friends called him IQ for short. IQ was a whiz on the computer. And he invented all of the super-cool gadgets Mary-Kate and Ashley used on their missions.

Mary-Kate flipped open her special-agent bracelet. "Misty to IQ." She spoke into the bracelet's tiny phone. "Are you there, IQ?"

"I'm here!" IQ said.

"We need any information you can find about Danny and Donnie Richards and the Quick Food restaurant," Mary-Kate told him. "Bring the info to the Quick Food on Fifth Street and Maple Avenue."

"I'm on it," IQ said. "See you soon, special agents!"

"IQ should be here any second," Ashley said. She looked through the window of the Quick Food restaurant. There were tons of customers inside talking, laughing, and eating.

"There he is!" Mary-Kate said, pointing to a boy with spiky brown hair rushing toward them.

"Hi, special agents," IQ said. "Here's the information you asked for." He handed Ashley a thick folder.

"So what's our next step?" Rod asked, leaning against the restaurant window.

"Why don't you get some food samples?" Mary-Kate said. "In the meantime, Ashley and I will look over the information IQ brought us."

"I'll get them!" IQ said. "I heard the food here is really good."

Ashley rolled her eyes. "Whatever," she said. "Just make sure you bring back one of everything they serve."

"Got it." IQ nodded and ran into the restaurant.

Ashley opened the folder that IQ had brought her. "It says here that Danny and Donnie almost never get along," she read.

"Really?" Mary-Kate said. "They seemed to get along on TV."

"Well, they are always fighting." Ashley read on. "In fact, their parents bought them this restaurant because they were hoping it would make Danny and Donnie work together."

Mary-Kate looked at the report over Ashley's shoulder. "It also says that Danny and Donnie's favorite subject is chemistry."

Ashley flipped through the folder. It

was filled with lots of information. It even had facts about different fast-food restaurants all across the country.

Ashley read through the whole thing. She loved interesting facts. She never knew when one of them would come in handy during a secret mission.

"Hey, guys, listen to this!" Ashley said. "According to this report, the average American eats fast food at least six times every month! That *can't* be healthy."

"I think that number is going up. Way up," Mary-Kate said. She nodded toward the line in front of Quick Food. "Look! It's even longer now than it was before lunch!"

How do Danny and Donnie get all these people to keep coming back? Ashley wondered. She thought for a second.

"Hey!" she said. "If Danny and Donnie are so good at chemistry, maybe they

know how to make secret ingredients. What if they are putting something in the food that makes everyone want to eat at Quick Food?"

"It could be," Mary-Kate said. "But we'll know for sure once IQ gets here with our food."

Mary-Kate looked at her watch. "What's taking him so long in there?"

"I guess the service at Quick Food isn't quick after all," Rod joked.

"Hey, here he comes!" Quincy barked.

The door to the restaurant swung open. IQ walked out carrying a white paper bag full of food. He was also chomping on a hamburger.

Mary-Kate and Ashley rushed up to him. "Did you get everything we asked for?"

"Yup," IQ said. "Tacos, pizza, spring rolls, fried chicken, hot dogs . . ." He turned to Ashley. "Did you know they even have Japanese food in there?"

Ashley frowned. "Why are you eating the evidence?" she asked.

"I couldn't help it!" IQ said. "It smelled so good. Besides, they gave me this Quick Patty for free." He popped the last piece of burger into his mouth.

Mary-Kate grabbed the bag from IQ's hand. "Come on. Let's check this stuff out."

Ashley lifted a taco from the bag and

unwrapped it. She took a big whiff. "Smells like any other taco," she said.

"Quincy," Mary-Kate said, "can your computer figure out what is in the taco?"

Quincy grabbed the taco in his mouth. Then he swallowed it with one huge gulp.

"Well?" Rod asked.

Quincy licked his lips. "Deee-licious!"

"We don't care how it tastes!" Mary-Kate said. "What's the secret ingredient?"

"Oh, right," Quincy said. His super-fast computer whirred inside him. "There isn't one. All I can see is ground beef, cheddar cheese, lettuce, tomato, and"—he burped—"extra-spicy salsa. Does anybody have a breath mint?"

Ashley ignored Quincy's question. She fed him the rest of the food. But Quincy didn't find any secret ingredients in the chicken, spring rolls, pizza, or hot dogs, either.

"I guess there must be another reason everyone keeps coming back to Quick Food," Mary-Kate said.

Ashley nodded. "And there's only one way to find out what it is. Special Agents Misty and Amber are going undercover!"

"Digital diary: Wednesday, three-thirty P.M." Mary-Kate whispered into her secret-agent bracelet. "It's our first day undercover at Quick Food. So far, we've seen nothing strange."

Mary-Kate looked down at her ugly red-and-blue uniform. "Well, except for this outfit!"

Ashley giggled and fixed her paper hat. "Time to get back to work."

Mary-Kate sighed. She took her place behind her cash register.

Ashley stood at a register next to Mary-Kate's. Soon a woman with light brown hair stepped up to the counter.

"Welcome to Quick Food." Ashley smiled at the woman. "May I take your order?"

"Yes!" the woman said. "I'll have an order of sushi, some fried chicken, and a side of wontons to go, please."

"No problem." Ashley punched the order into the computer. Then she handed the woman her food. "That will be ten dollars and—"

"Wait a minute!" someone called.

Ashley whirled around. Donnie and Danny Richards were running toward her.

"Wait! Her free Quick Patty!" Donnie

said. He handed the customer a burger.

"*Never* let the customer leave without getting a free Quick Patty!" Danny said.

"How do you stay in business if you give away so much free food?" Mary-Kate asked.

Danny glanced at Donnie and smiled.

Donnie slowly smiled back. "Those free Quick Patties help bring back business in a *big* way," he said.

Whoa! Ashley thought. *What did*

Donnie mean by that? Was there some-thing the brothers weren't telling them?

The next customer stepped up. "Can I have one Quick Dog and one slice of pizza?" he asked.

Ashley looked at the customer. It was IQ!

"IQ!" she said. "What are you doing here?"

IQ shrugged. "I love Quick Food so much," he said.

"Are you kidding?" Ashley asked. "Quick Food is under investigation!"

"I know, I know," IQ said. "But I can't help it. I *have* to eat here."

"Says who?" Mary-Kate asked.

"Says my stomach!" IQ replied, rubbing his belly.

"This is reminding me of something," Mary-Kate whispered.

"What is it?" Ashley asked.

"Remember when we had to stop the evil Renee La Rouge from making mind-control makeup?" Mary-Kate asked.

"Yes," Ashley said. "That was one of our toughest missions ever!"

"Whenever someone put on the makeup, they had to do whatever Renee wanted," Mary-Kate said.

"So what does that have to do with IQ?" Ashley asked.

"Maybe IQ is being controlled by the food here!" Mary-Kate said.

"No way," Ashley said. "We checked all the food yesterday. There are no secret ingredients." She handed IQ his order.

"Don't forget his free Quick Patty!" Donnie called as he walked by.

His free Quick Patty, Ashley thought slowly. "I was wrong," she said. "We *didn't* check all the food!"

"That's right!" Mary-Kate agreed. "IQ

had already eaten the free Quick Patty before Quincy could taste it."

Ashley handed IQ a Quick Patty. "*Don't eat this,*" she said. "Give it to Quincy. He'll figure out what's in it."

"You got it," IQ said, his mouth already full of hot dog. He turned and left the restaurant.

Ashley smiled at Mary-Kate. She had a feeling they were about to uncover Danny and Donnie's evil plan!

Headquarters on her special-agent bracelet. "What did you find out?" she asked IQ.

"We didn't uncover a mind-controlling ingredient," IQ said through the speaker. "But there *was* an ingredient that Quincy's computer couldn't identify."

Ashley and Mary-Kate looked at each other.

"What could it be?" Ashley asked.

"I don't know," Mary-Kate said. "But tomorrow we're going to find out!"

CHAPTER FOUR
Double Danger

The next morning Mary-Kate and Ashley walked toward the Quick Food restaurant.

"Ready to find that missing ingredient?" Ashley asked.

"You bet!" Mary-Kate cheered.

"Hey, Misty! Amber! Wait up!"

Ashley turned to see Danny jogging toward her. "That's weird," she said. "Danny always gets to work super-early."

"How come you're not at Quick Food?" Mary-Kate asked Danny.

"Because I'm not working at Quick Food anymore," Danny said.

"You're not?" Ashley cried.

Danny shook his head. "Donnie and I have so many customers that we are

opening another restaurant. Take a look."
He pointed to a sparkling new restaurant
across the street. It looked exactly the
same as Quick Food!

"This restaurant is called Quicker
Food," Danny said. "I'm going to need
some help running it. Misty, do you want
to be my manager?"

"Sure!" Mary-Kate said. She leaned toward her sister. "We'd better split up," she whispered. "That way I can stick close to Danny and you can keep an eye on Donnie."

"Good idea!" Ashley said. She handed Mary-Kate a mini-camera. "Hide this in Danny's kitchen. I'm going to hide one in Donnie's kitchen. That way, we can watch both brothers at all times."

"Got it," Mary-Kate said.

"What's going on?" Donnie called from the door of Quick Food. He strolled over.

"I just hired Misty to work at Quicker Food," Danny said.

"What!" Donnie folded his arms. "Why are you stealing my employees?"

"I didn't think you would mind," Danny said.

"That's not true," Donnie said. "I bet you just want to make sure that your restaurant is better than my restaurant."

Danny narrowed his eyes. "I *know* my restaurant will be better."

"Will not!"

"Will too!"

"We'll just see about that!" Donnie said. "Let's go, Amber." He marched into Quick Food. Ashley said good-bye to Mary-Kate and followed.

"He wants our parents to think I can't run my own restaurant!" Donnie said. "That way, they'll love him more!"

Ashley placed a hand on Donnie's shoulder. "No way, Donnie. My parents wouldn't love me less if I wasn't as smart or as good at things as my sister."

"Really? Then why did Misty jump at the chance to become Danny's manager?" Donnie asked.

Ashley shrugged. She couldn't tell Donnie the *real* reason Mary-Kate had taken the job. She decided to make up an excuse.

"He gave her a better job," Ashley said. "Why would she say no to that?"

"Well, don't worry, Amber," Donnie said. "I'm making you the new manager of Quick Food! That is, if you want to be the manager."

"Sure," Ashley said.

"Great!" Donnie cheered. "Then let's get to work!"

That night, Mary-Kate and Ashley slumped into chairs at the Chow Family Restaurant. Rod, IQ, and Quincy were already at the table.

"I am totally wiped out!" Ashley

groaned. "Being a manager stinks. I spent eight hours cleaning up spills and carrying in food deliveries. I even had to haul a bottle of ketchup that was practically as tall as I am!"

"Sounds just like my day," Mary-Kate said.

"Did you find out what the secret ingredient is?" IQ asked.

"No!" Ashley said. "We searched everywhere. But we couldn't find anything that wasn't regular food."

Uncle Frank hurried over to the table with a platter of steaming food.

"Forget about Quick Food for a minute," Rod said. "I'm hungry. Let's dig in!"

Ashley passed a plate filled with food to IQ. "No, thanks," he said. "I had a big lunch at Quick Food before I got here."

"IQ!" Mary-Kate said. "Why do you keep eating there?"

"Because the food is sooo good!" IQ said.

"It is pretty good," Ashley admitted. "I had some for lunch."

Mary-Kate nodded slowly. "I wasn't going to tell you," she said, "but I've been snacking on the French fries all day."

"Well, I'm starving!" Quincy said. "Pass the chicken."

"Are you sure you want it?" Rod asked. "There are sesame seeds in there."

"We know how much you hate sesame seeds, Quincy," Mary-Kate said.

"It's okay," Quincy said. "IQ fixed my computer a few days ago so that I can't even taste them anymore."

Ashley looked at Mary-Kate. Mary-Kate looked at Ashley.

"Hold on a second," Ashley said. "You're saying that if you ate something with sesame seeds in it, your computer wouldn't recognize them?"

"That's right," Quincy said.

"Did IQ fix your computer before or after you analyzed the food samples for us?" Mary-Kate said.

"Before," Quincy replied. "Why?"

Mary-Kate slapped her forehead. "The Quick Patty you ate yesterday had a sesame seed bun!" she said. "That must be the ingredient your computer couldn't identify!"

IQ froze with his glass halfway to his mouth. "Oops," he said. "I guess I should have thought of that."

Ashley sighed. "Let's face it," she said. "We have no idea what Danny and Donnie are up to at Quick Food."

"Maybe they're up to nothing," Mary-Kate said quietly. "Maybe their food is just that good!"

"And when you factor in the free

burgers that Danny and Donnie are giving away," IQ said, "lots of people are going to eat there for sure!"

Ashley thought about it. Mary-Kate and IQ were right. Danny and Donnie were running a regular business. They were just doing it really well!

"I guess that's the end of our mission," Mary-Kate said.

Ashley glumly picked up her fork. She was about to spear a piece of broccoli when—

"Aaaaaah!"

Ashley jumped. Someone outside was screaming!

"What's going on?" Rod asked.

Uncle Frank ran to the window. "It's coming from Quick Food," he said. "And it looks like trouble!"

Ashley glanced at Mary-Kate. Maybe their mission *wasn't* over yet!

CHAPTER FIVE

Food Fight

Mary-Kate and Ashley rushed out of
the restaurant. A white cloud floated
around Quick Food's front door.

"Is that smoke?" Ashley asked. "Is
there a fire?"

"No," Mary-Kate answered. "Look!"

Donnie staggered out the front door. He was covered in flour from head to toe. "I don't believe this!" he said.

Donnie stomped across the street and banged on the front door of Danny's restaurant. "Get out here, you shrimp! I want to talk to you!"

Danny walked out of his restaurant. "Ha, ha, ha!" He pointed at his brother. "You look so funny! I knew you would fall for my trick."

Mary-Kate and Ashley walked over.

"What did you do, Danny?" Ashley asked.

"I put a big bag of flour on top of Donnie's refrigerator," Danny said. "So when he opened the door the flour fell all over him!"

Danny laughed even harder.

Mary-Kate giggled. Ashley elbowed her in the ribs.

"Sorry," Mary-Kate whispered, "but that *is* funny!"

"You keep laughing, Danny," Donnie said. "I'll show you what's funny!" He stomped back into his restaurant.

"Uh-oh," Ashley whispered. "Looks like trouble."

Mary-Kate nodded. "This could get ugly."

"Why did you play a trick on Donnie?" Ashley asked Danny.

"Donnie always thinks he's better than I am," Danny said. "Now it's time for me to get even!"

"Hey, Danny!" Donnie called from outside his restaurant. "Don't forget the fries you ordered!"

SPLAT! SPLAT! SPLAT! Hundreds of French fries flew across the street. They hit Mary-Kate, Ashley, and Danny.

"Stop it!" Mary-Kate yelled. She held her hands in front of her face.

Grease dripped down Ashley's cheek.
"Gross!" she yelled.

"I'll get you for that, big brother!"
Danny shook his fist at Donnie.

"But first, how about a little ketchup
with those fries?" Donnie called.

Ashley glanced up and saw Donnie dragging a huge ketchup bottle onto the sidewalk. He set it on the ground with the end pointing right at Quicker Food. Then he leaped into the air and landed on the bottle with both feet.

SPLOOSH! A wave of ketchup shot across the street. Ashley stared down at her clothes. They were covered in sticky red ketchup!

"Yuck!" Mary-Kate yelled. "I look like . . ."

". . . you fell in a giant pile of tomatoes?" Ashley finished. Both girls began to giggle.

"There's nothing funny about this!" Danny yelled. He hurried back into his restaurant.

A moment later, a delivery truck skidded to a stop in front of Quicker Food. Danny opened the back door of the truck.

Ashley gasped. The truck was filled with chocolate cream pies!

"This does not look good," she said.

Danny began flinging pies across the street at his brother.

Splat! One of the pies hit Donnie square in the face.

"That's it, Danny," Donnie said. He wiped some cream off his shirt. "You asked for it!"

He turned and disappeared inside his restaurant. A second later he returned carrying a huge slingshot.

"Take a bite of this!" Donnie yelled. He loaded the giant hamburger display into the slingshot and flung it at his brother.

"Oof!" The burger knocked Danny to the ground.

"This is crazy!" Mary-Kate cried. "Do you think they'll *ever* stop?"

Ashley frowned. "Maybe . . . when they run out of food!"

"This is totally gross!" Ashley said later that night. She looked at the street in front of her. It was completely covered in food.

"We may never see the sidewalk again," Mary-Kate agreed.

Rod, IQ, and Quincy walked up to Mary-Kate and Ashley.

"Cool!" Quincy said. "It's like a big doggie buffet out here!"

"Are you two okay?" IQ asked.

Ashley nodded. "It looks like Danny and Donnie put each other out of business," she said.

"Which means that the Chow Family Restaurant will get its customers back," Rod said.

Ashley glanced at Quick Food. "I know our mission is over," she said, "but maybe there's something else we can do."

"What do you mean?" Mary-Kate asked.

"Maybe we can help Danny and Donnie stop fighting with each other," Ashley said.

"That's a great idea!" Mary-Kate said. "Let's do it!"

CHAPTER SIX

"Hi, girls," Donnie greeted Mary-Kate and Ashley as they walked into Quick Food a few hours later.

"Hi, Donnie," Ashley said. "We want to talk to you."

"No problem," Donnie said. "What's it all about?"

"It's about your brother." Mary-Kate folded her arms. "Donnie, do you two always have to be so mean to each other?" she asked.

"Yes," Donnie said.

"You know, if the two of you stopped trying to outdo each other, you might get along better," Mary-Kate pointed out. "You might even be able to have fun together."

Donnie started to chuckle. "You know what was fun? Seeing Danny's face when I hit him with that giant burger."

"Danny doesn't think it's very funny," Ashley said.

"That's right," Mary-Kate said. "We were just over there, talking to him. He's sitting in his kitchen, totally bummed."

Donnie looked up. "Really?" he asked.

"See for yourself," Ashley said. She pulled out her special-agent bracelet.

"Misty planted a tiny camera in his restaurant."

She pressed a button and the bracelet's small screen blinked on.

Ashley gasped when she saw what was on the screen. The picture showed Danny flapping his arms—trying to stay afloat in a kitchen full of water!

"Oh, no!" she said.

Donnie and Mary-Kate leaned in.

"What is going on in there?" Mary-Kate asked.

Donnie hid his face in his hands. "This is all my fault!"

"Donnie, what did you do?" Ashley asked.

"I greased all the doorknobs—and the faucets! He can't turn the water off or open the doors! All the knobs are too slippery," Donnie said. "It was just supposed to be a joke. I never meant to hurt him!"

"Come on!" Ashley said. "We've got to get Danny out of there before he drowns!"

Mary-Kate, Ashley, and Donnie raced across the street. They stopped when they reached the side door of Quicker Food, which led into the kitchen.

Mary-Kate pulled on the knob. "It's

locked!" she said. "What do we do now?"

"Don't worry," Ashley said. "I read a book on how to pick locks. I'll have this open in no time!"

"Wow," Mary-Kate said. "You really *do* know random facts about everything!"

Ashley pulled a bobby pin from her hair. Within a few seconds, she had the door unlocked.

WHOOSH! The door flew open. A wall of water gushed out. It swept Ashley, Mary-Kate, and Donnie onto the sidewalk.

Danny tumbled out after them. He sat on the curb, coughing and sputtering.

"Danny! I'm so glad you're all right!" Donnie ran to his brother and locked him in a bear hug.

"So am I," a man's voice said.

Ashley looked up. Standing over her were IQ, Rod—and a man and a woman she had never seen before.

"Dad?" Donnie asked. "Mom?"

"What are you doing here?" Danny gulped.

"We came to see how the restaurant is doing," Mr. Richards said.

"You boys are in big trouble," Mrs. Richards said. "Rod and IQ filled us in on everything."

"W-we can explain!" Danny said.

"There will be plenty of time for that," Mr. Richards said. "You two are grounded. *And* you're fired."

"What?" Danny and Donnie shouted.

"That's right," Mrs. Richards said. "We gave you that restaurant so that you could learn to get along."

"But you wound up fighting even more." Mr. Richards shook his head. "You boys are *family*. You have to learn to work *together*."

"You're right," Donnie said.

"I agree," Danny said. "Brothers

shouldn't fight." He gave Donnie another hug.

"Boy, all this excitement has made me hungry," Mary-Kate said.

"Well, I know a great place for a snack," Ashley said. "Follow me!"

A few minutes later, the whole group was seated at a big round table in the Chow Family Restaurant. Aunt Jane hurried to get everyone menus.

"Looks like this mission is over," Ashley said to Mary-Kate. "We rescued Danny from drowning!"

"Plus, Danny and Donnie learned an important lesson about family," Mary-Kate added.

Aunt Jane returned with the menus and tossed Quincy a fortune cookie. Quincy smashed the cookie with his paw. Then he picked up the fortune in his teeth and dropped it in Ashley's hand.

Ashley smiled as she glanced at the slip of paper. "Here's the real secret to running a good restaurant," she said.

"What is it?" Danny asked.

"'Good food tastes better with good family,'" Ashley read.

"That is so true!" Mary-Kate said, giving her sister a huge hug.

CALENDARS

POSTERS

live your style

BOOKS

VIDEOGAMES

TELEVISION

MARY-KATE AND ASHLEY iN ACTiON!

ON

TOON DISNEY CHANNEL

DUALSTAR CONSUMER PRODUCTS

mary-kateandashley.com
America Online Keyword: mary-kateandashley

mary-kateandashley
LET US ENTERTAIN YOU

VIDEOS AND DVDs

CDs

BOARDGAME

DOLLS

Win

MARY-KATE AND ASHLEY in ACTION!

Dolls!

75 lucky Grand Prize winners will win *Mary-Kate and Ashley in ACTION!* Dolls

It's
What
YOU
Read

Mail to: *MARY-KATE AND ASHLEY in ACTION!*
DOLL SWEEPSTAKES
c/o HarperEntertainment
Attention: Children's Marketing Department
10 East 53rd Street
New York, NY 10022

No purchase necessary.

Name: _____

Address: _____

City: _____ State: _____ Zip: _____

Phone: _____ Age: _____

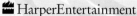